Lulu's Pajamas

Written by Lucie Papineau
Illustrated by Stéphane Jorisch

KIDS CAN PRESS

My name is Lulu.

This is Mama and Papa, the best mama and papa in the world. And this, of course, is Lili-poo, my one and only ladybug.

When it is time to go to bed, I put on my
favorite pajamas. They smell as good as a pink
dream. They are as soft as a butterfly kiss.

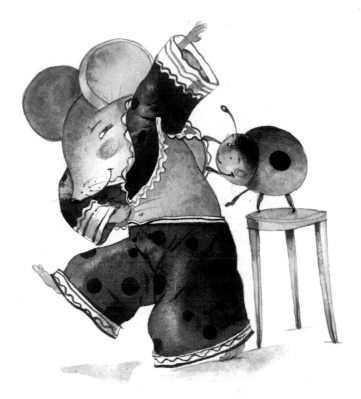

Then Mama tells us a story. Papa sings us
a good-night song. And I go to sleep in my
soft-as-a-butterfly-kiss pajamas … with Lili-poo,
who *never* wears pajamas!

One morning, I make a BIG decision: I will never take off my soft-as-a-butterfly-kiss pajamas. Never ever!

I say "No, no, no!" when Mama brings me my clothes. I say "No, no, no!" when Papa tells me to put them on. I kick my feet and I cry.

Mama and Papa look at each other. They make a big decision, too.

Papa drives me to school … wearing his pajamas!
My friends laugh when they see us. I want to kick my
feet and cry again. So does Lili-poo.

Luckily, Miss Mimi rings her bell and puts
a finger to her lips: "Shhh!"

In Miss Mimi's classroom, we have lots of fun. We finger paint. Oops! Some paint gets on my pajama sleeves.

We make caterpillars. Oops! Some glue drops on my pajama buttons.

We do the elf-and-fairy dance.
Oops! My pajama seat is very dusty!

When I go home for lunch, I eat spaghetti with red tomatoes, yellow cheese, brown mushrooms and green zucchinis.

Oops! All the colors end up on
my pajamas ... and on Lili-poo!

By the end of the afternoon, my pajamas don't even look like my favorite pajamas anymore. They have a tear at the knee. They don't smell like a pink dream. They are not as soft as a butterfly kiss.

Lili-poo is sad. So am I.

I make another BIG decision: I will never wear my
soft-as-a-butterfly-kiss pajamas again. Never ever!

"All right," says Mama.

"Good idea," says Papa.

We all take off our pajamas … except Lili-poo,
who is not wearing any!

When night falls, I go to bed wearing my orange ballerina dress. Mama tucks me in and then turns off the light.

"Mama, Mama! You forgot something!"

"Hmm ... I don't think so," answers Mama.

"What about our story? And Papa's song?"

Mama winks at me. "I only tell stories to little mice
who wear pajamas," she says.

"And I only sing songs to little mice who wear pajamas," adds Papa.
I frown. Then I look at Lili-poo. She knows *everything*. So I start thinking.

Finally I make one more BIG decision: I will only wear my favorite pajamas *some* of the time! After a long day at school, they don't smell like a pink dream anymore. And they are not as soft as a butterfly kiss.

But my pajamas are perfect for listening to bedtime stories and good-night songs, and for dreaming sweet dreams.

"Right, Lili-poo?"

To Marie-Louise Gay — L.P.

To Emma and Olivia — S.J.

Originally published under the title *Tulipe Mon pyjama à moi* by Dominique et Compagnie

Text © 2009 Lucie Papineau
Illustrations © 2009 Stéphane Jorisch
English translation © 2009 Marie-Louise Gay

Kids Can Press acknowledges the financial support of the Government of Ontario, through the Ontario Media Development Corporation's Ontario Book Initiative; the Ontario Arts Council; the Canada Council for the Arts; and the Government of Canada, through the BPIDP, for our publishing activity.

Published in Canada by
Kids Can Press Ltd.
29 Birch Avenue
Toronto, ON M4V 1E2

Published in the U.S. by
Kids Can Press Ltd.
2250 Military Road
Tonawanda, NY 14150

www.kidscanpress.com

The artwork in this book was rendered in watercolor.
The text is set in Usherwood Book.

Edited by Tara Walker
Designed by Karen Powers
Printed and bound in China

This book is smyth sewn casebound.

CM 09 0 9 8 7 6 5 4 3 2 1

Library and Archives Canada Cataloguing in Publication

Papineau, Lucie
[Mon pyjama à moi. English]
    Lulu's pajamas / written by Lucie Papineau ; illustrated by Stéphane Jorisch.

Translation of: Mon pyjama à moi.

I. Jorisch, Stéphane II. Title. III. Title: Mon pyjama à moi. English.

PS8581.A6658M6513 2009   jC843'.54   C2008-907835-7

Kids Can Press is a **corus**™ Entertainment company

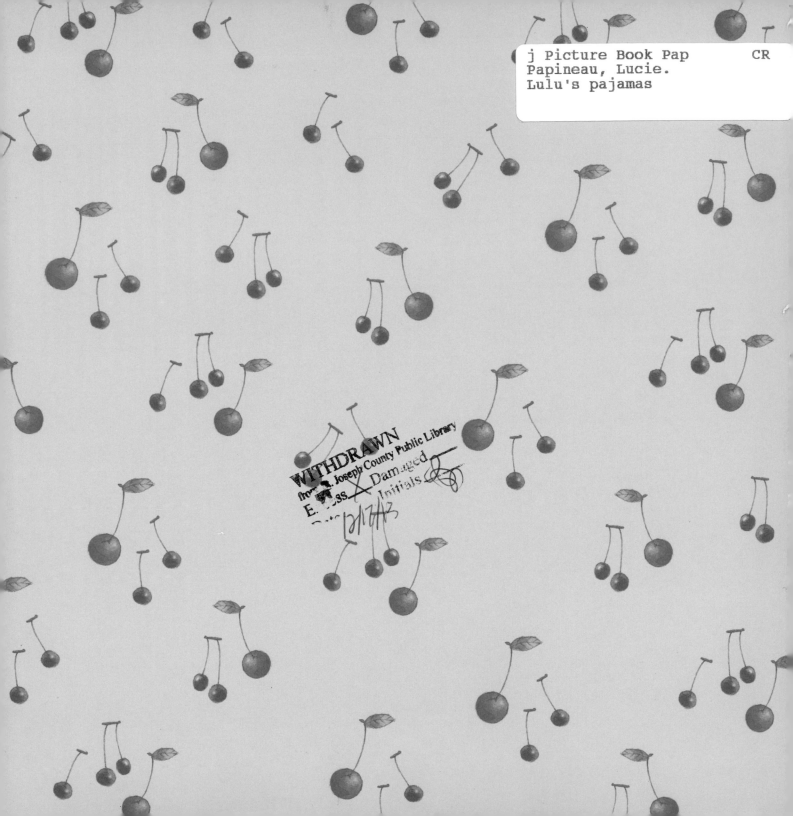